W9-CYF-033

WITHDRAWN

VIRGINIA

Sarah Tieck

Big Buddy BOOKS
Explore the United States

Published by ABDO Publishing Company, PO Box 398166, Minneapolis, MN 55439.

Printed in the United States of America, North Mankato, Minnesota.
052012
092012

 PRINTED ON RECYCLED PAPER

Coordinating Series Editor: Rochelle Baltzer
Contributing Editors: Megan M. Gunderson, Marcia Zappa
Graphic Design: Adam Craven
Cover Photograph: *Shutterstock*: Mary Terriberry.
Interior Photographs/Illustrations: *Alamy*: North Wind Picture Archives (p. 13); *AP Photo*: AP Photo (p. 23), Cal Sport Media via AP Images (p. 27), Steve Helber (p. 26), North Wind Picture Archives via AP Images (p. 13); *Getty Images*: Annie Griffiths Belt/National Geographic (p. 29), Superstock (p. 25); *iStockphoto*: ©iStockphoto.com/ Coast-to-Coast (p. 26), ©iStockphoto.com/DoxaDigital (p. 9), ©iStockphoto.com/keithpix (p. 5), ©iStockphoto. com/Lingbeek (p. 17), ©iStockphoto.com/Montes-Bradley (p. 25), ©iStockphoto.com/nojustice (pp. 9, 21), ©iStockphoto.com/SochAnam (p. 19); *Shutterstock*: PAUL ATKINSON (p. 30), L. Kragt Bakker (p. 27), Steve Byland (p. 30), Carolyn M Carpenter (p. 23), Frontpage (p. 19), Philip Lange (p. 30), Caitlin Mirra (p. 27), Steven Russell Smith Photos (p. 30), trekandshoot (p. 11).

All population figures taken from the 2010 US census.

Library of Congress Cataloging-in-Publication Data

Tieck, Sarah, 1976-
 Virginia / Sarah Tieck.
    p. cm. -- (Explore the United States)
 ISBN 978-1-61783-385-4
 1. Virginia--Juvenile literature. I. Title.
 F226.3.T54 2013
 975.5--dc23
                         2012017451

VIRGINIA

Contents

One Nation 4

Virginia Up Close 6

Important Cities 8

Virginia in History 12

Timeline 14

Across the Land 16

Earning a Living 18

Natural Wonder 20

Hometown Heroes 22

Tour Book 26

A Great State 28

Fast Facts 30

Important Words 31

Web Sites 31

Index 32

ONE NATION

The United States is a **diverse** country. It has farmland, cities, coasts, and mountains. Its people come from many different backgrounds. And, its history covers more than 200 years.

Today the country includes 50 states. Virginia is one of these states. Let's learn more about Virginia and its story!

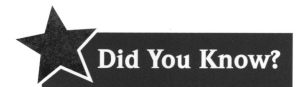

Did You Know?

Virginia became a state on June 25, 1788. It was the tenth state to join the nation.

Virginia is home to parts of the Blue Ridge Mountains.

VIRGINIA UP CLOSE

The United States has four main **regions**. Virginia is in the South.

Virginia has five states on its borders. Maryland is northeast. West Virginia is northwest. Kentucky is west. Tennessee and North Carolina are south. The Atlantic Ocean is east.

Virginia has a total area of 40,599 square miles (105,151 sq km). About 8 million people live there.

REGIONS OF THE UNITED STATES

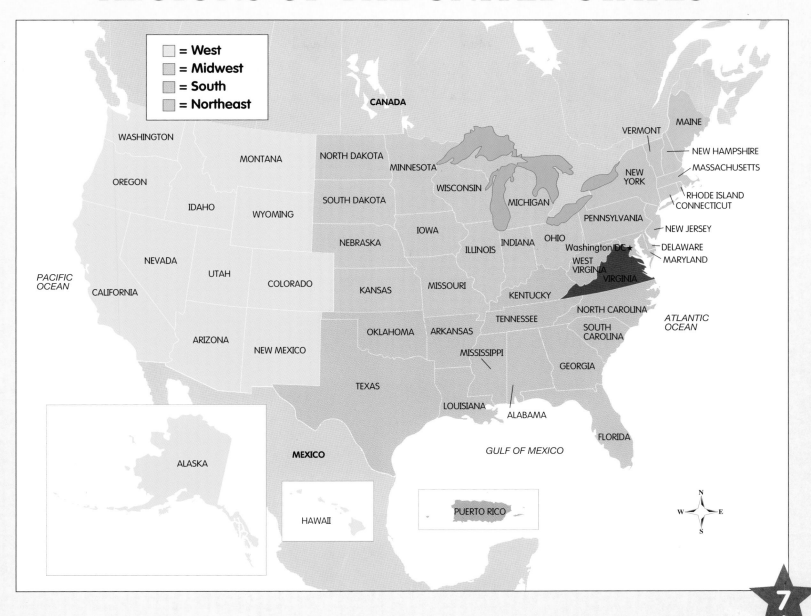

= West
= Midwest
= South
= Northeast

CANADA

WASHINGTON
MONTANA
OREGON
IDAHO
WYOMING
NORTH DAKOTA
MINNESOTA
SOUTH DAKOTA
WISCONSIN
MICHIGAN
NEVADA
UTAH
COLORADO
IOWA
NEBRASKA
ILLINOIS
INDIANA
OHIO
CALIFORNIA
ARIZONA
NEW MEXICO
KANSAS
MISSOURI
OKLAHOMA
ARKANSAS
TEXAS
LOUISIANA
MISSISSIPPI
ALABAMA

VERMONT
MAINE
NEW HAMPSHIRE
MASSACHUSETTS
NEW YORK
RHODE ISLAND
CONNECTICUT
PENNSYLVANIA
NEW JERSEY
Washington DC ★
DELAWARE
MARYLAND
WEST VIRGINIA
VIRGINIA
KENTUCKY
NORTH CAROLINA
TENNESSEE
SOUTH CAROLINA
GEORGIA
FLORIDA

PACIFIC OCEAN
ATLANTIC OCEAN

ALASKA

MEXICO

HAWAII

PUERTO RICO

GULF OF MEXICO

N
W   E
S

7

IMPORTANT CITIES

Richmond is Virginia's **capital**. The James River flows through this historic city. The Virginia Historical Society is located there. It has a large collection of objects and papers from the state's beginning.

Virginia Beach is the state's largest city, with 437,994 people. This city is on the Atlantic Ocean. It is a popular vacation spot.

Virginia

Richmond ★

Norfolk
Chesapeake
Virginia Beach

The Virginia State Capitol was designed by Thomas Jefferson. It was completed in 1788.

People spend time playing in the sand and walking the boardwalks in Virginia Beach.

Norfolk is Virginia's second-largest city, with 242,803 people. Chesapeake Bay and the Elizabeth River border the city.

The third-largest city in the state is Chesapeake. It is home to 222,209 people. Part of the Dismal **Swamp** is in this city.

Did You Know?

Some say famous poet Edgar Allan Poe wrote parts of his poem "The Raven" while visiting the Dismal Swamp.

Norfolk is at the mouth of Chesapeake Bay.

Virginia in History

Virginia's history includes Native Americans, colonists, and war. Native Americans were the first to live in present-day Virginia. In 1607, the Jamestown Colony was established there. This was the first lasting English settlement in North America.

By 1775, colonists no longer wanted to be ruled by England. So, they fought in the **Revolutionary War** and formed the United States. Virginia became a state in 1788.

John Smith was one of the leaders of the Jamestown Colony.

Jamestown colonists lived off the land. It was a hard life. Many faced hunger and sickness.

13

Timeline

1776

Thomas Jefferson of Shadwell wrote the **Declaration of Independence**.

1788

Virginia became the tenth state.

1861

Richmond became the **capital** of the Southern states during the **American Civil War**.

1700s

1800s

England's troops **surrendered** to General George Washington at Yorktown. This meant America had won the **Revolutionary War**.

Washington became the first US president.

1789

Southern soldiers surrendered at Appomattox Court House. This was an important step toward ending the American Civil War.

1865

1781

1989

1912

Douglas Wilder of Richmond became the first African American to be elected governor in the United States.

2011

Woodrow Wilson became the eighth person from Virginia to serve as US president.

A very strong earthquake struck near Richmond.

1900s

2000s

Virginia schools started to integrate. This meant students of all races attended the same schools.

In Arlington County, a plane crashed into the Pentagon on September 11. This was part of the worst terrorist attack in US history.

1959

2001

ACROSS THE LAND

Virginia has mountains, hills, valleys, **swamps**, rivers, and coasts. The Blue Ridge Mountains are in the western part of the state. Virginia borders the Atlantic Ocean and Chesapeake Bay. Its major rivers include the Potomac and the Shenandoah.

Many types of animals make their homes in Virginia. These include black bears, ducks, and rabbits. Oysters live in the coastal waters.

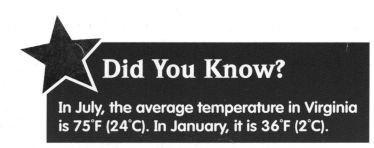

Did You Know?

In July, the average temperature in Virginia is 75°F (24°C). In January, it is 36°F (2°C).

The Shenandoah Valley is famous for its beauty.

EARNING A LIVING

Virginia has many important businesses. Some people work in factories that make beverages, food products, and medicines. Others work in government jobs or help visitors to the state.

Virginia's land provides important products. Coal and stone come from the state's mines. Tobacco is a leading product of Virginia's farms. Tomatoes, beans, and potatoes also grow there. And, fishermen catch scallops in the state's coastal waters.

Chickens, turkeys, and cattle are some of the livestock raised in Virginia.

Northeast Virginia is near the US capital, Washington DC. The state is home to the Pentagon (*below*) and other government offices.

19

NATURAL WONDER

Virginia is known for its natural beauty. The Dismal **Swamp** is one of the largest swamps in the United States. It covers about 750 square miles (2,000 sq km) of land in Virginia and North Carolina. Visitors enjoy hiking and biking in this area.

The Dismal Swamp has hanging vines and many different types of trees. Opossums, gray foxes, bears, and white-tailed deer live there.

The Dismal Swamp Canal is on the eastern side of the swamp. It has been used to move goods and people since the 1800s.

21

HOMETOWN HEROES

Many famous people are from Virginia. George Washington was born in Westmoreland County in 1732. He led American soldiers during the **Revolutionary War**. With his help, America became a new nation.

Washington was also the first US president. He served from 1789 to 1797. The government he helped build is still strong today. Washington is called "the Father of the Country."

Washington's home is called Mount Vernon. More than 1 million people visit it each year.

Washington was known for being a strong leader.

23

Thomas Jefferson was born in Shadwell in 1743. He wrote the **Declaration of Independence**. And, he was an important leader during the **Revolutionary War**.

In 1801, Jefferson became the third US president. He arranged for the **Louisiana Purchase** in 1803. He served until 1809. Later, Jefferson founded the University of Virginia in Charlottesville.

Did You Know?

Virginia is called "the Mother of Presidents." Eight US presidents were born there! These include James Madison, James Monroe, William Henry Harrison, John Tyler, Zachary Taylor, and Woodrow Wilson.

Jefferson never fought in the Revolutionary War. Instead, he worked in the government.

Jefferson's home is called Monticello. People can visit this famous building.

Tour Book

Do you want to go to Virginia? If you visit the state, here are some places to go and things to do!

 **Play**

Take a boat ride on the James River! People canoe and raft on its fast-moving waters.

 Discover

At Jamestown Settlement, see copies of the ships that carried settlers to the Jamestown Colony. And, get a look at what life was like when the colony began.

 # Remember

Walk through historic buildings in Colonial Williamsburg. Costumed actors show what life was like in the 1700s. At that time, Williamsburg was Virginia colony's capital.

 # Cheer

Watch a football or basketball game. The University of Virginia and Virginia Tech both have popular teams.

 # See

Take a ride on Skyline Drive. This road in the Blue Ridge Mountains offers views of the Shenandoah Valley.

A Great State

The story of Virginia is important to the United States. The people and places that make up this state offer something special to the country. Together with all the states, Virginia helps make the United States great.

Virginia's flowering dogwood trees bloom in the spring.

Fast Facts

Date of Statehood:
June 25, 1788

State Capital:
Richmond

Postal Abbreviation:
VA

Population (rank):
8,001,024
(12th most-populated state)

Flag:

Tree: Flowering Dogwood

Total Area (rank):
40,599 square miles
(36th largest state)

Motto:
"Sic Semper Tyrannis"
(Thus Always to Tyrants)

Flower: Flowering Dogwood

Bird: Northern Cardinal

Nickname:
Mother of Presidents,
The Old Dominion

Important Words

American Civil War the war between the Northern and Southern states from 1861 to 1865.
capital a city where government leaders meet.
Declaration of Independence a very important paper in American history. It announces the separation of the American colonies from Great Britain.
diverse made up of things that are different from each other.
Louisiana Purchase land the United States purchased from France in 1803. It extended from the Mississippi River to the Rocky Mountains and from Canada through the Gulf of Mexico.
region a large part of a country that is different from other parts.
Revolutionary War a war fought between England and the North American colonies from 1775 to 1783.
surrender to give up.
swamp land that is wet and often covered with water.

Web Sites

To learn more about Virginia, visit ABDO Publishing Company online. Web sites about Virginia are featured on our Book Links page. These links are routinely monitored and updated to provide the most current information available.

www.abdopublishing.com

Index

American Civil War **14**
American colonies **12, 13, 26, 27**
animals **16, 20, 30**
Appomattox Court House **14**
Arlington County **15**
Atlantic Ocean **6, 8, 16**
Blue Ridge Mountains **5, 16, 27**
businesses **18, 19**
Charlottesville **24**
Chesapeake **10**
Chesapeake Bay **10, 11, 16**
Dismal Swamp **10, 20, 21**
Elizabeth River **10**
England **12, 14**
James River **8, 26**
Jefferson, Thomas **9, 14, 24, 25**
Monticello **25**
Mount Vernon **23**
Native Americans **12**
natural resources **18**
Norfolk **10, 11**

Pentagon **15, 19**
population **6, 8, 10, 30**
Potomac River **16**
Revolutionary War **12, 14, 22, 24, 25**
Richmond **8, 14, 15, 30**
Shadwell **14, 24**
Shenandoah River **16**
Shenandoah Valley **17, 27**
size **6, 30**
Smith, John **13**
South (region) **6**
statehood **4, 12, 14, 30**
Virginia Beach **8, 9**
Virginia Historical Society **8**
Washington, George **14, 22, 23**
weather **16**
Westmoreland County **22**
Wilder, Douglas **15**
Williamsburg **27**
Wilson, Woodrow **15, 24**
Yorktown **14**